HOT AIR

John Mole, whose collection *Boo to a Goose* won the Signal Award in 1988, is one of the leading poets writing for children today. His work for adults is also widely acclaimed and won a Cholmondeley Award in 1994. A teacher and editor for a small press, John Mole has compiled and presented feature programmes for the BBC. He also plays regularly as a jazz clarinettist. John Mole is married to the artist Mary Norman, has two sons, and lives in Hertfordshire.

Text copyright © John Mole 1996

The right of John Mole and Peter Bailey to be identified as the author and illustrator of the work has been asserted by them in accordance with the Copyright, Designs and Patents Act 1988.

Illustrations copyright © Peter Bailey 1996

Designed by Diane Thistlethwaite

Cover illustration by Tracey Morgan
Cover design by Vic Groombridge

Published by Hodder Children's Books 1996
10 9 8 7 6 5 4 3

ISBN 0340 65701 4

A Catalogue record for this book is available from the British Library.

Hodder Children's Books
A division of Hodder Headline plc
338 Euston Road
London NW1 3BH

Printed and bound by Cox & Wyman Ltd, Reading, Berks.

CONTENTS

THE BALLOON

It's all hot air they said
You'll never do it
But now the laugh's on them
As up and up I go
Beyond their ordinary world.

I look down, sorry
For the tilted faces
And those tiny handkerchiefs
Which wave together,
Proud of me at last.

Wherever I land
Will be different.
I shall step out
A qualified dreamer
With his feet on the ground.

FIRST LOVE

Everyone says that my girlfriend Gemma
Is big for her age
And that what we apparently feel for each other
Is only a stage.

But what, when they grumble, I have to agree
Is as plain as day
Is that Gemma tends to throw her big weight about
Every which way.

Once when I showed her a shed in our garden
She climbed on the roof
And then when I wasn't expecting leapt down
   like an Amazon.
Strewth!

All of my breath was completely knocked out of me,
All of my puff,
But just to have Gemma landing on top of me
Was enough.

TIME TO MAKE UP

You can lead a horse to water
But you cannot make it drink,
You can stare at a railway porter
But you'll never make him blink,
You can cut your homework shorter
But still you have to think.

You can change your socks each morning
But that won't shine your shoes,
You can leave home without warning
But you'll end up joining queues,
You can say you're only yawning
But they'll know you sing the blues.

You can hope this is for ever
But I'll sit near the phone,
You can reckon you've been clever
But now you're all alone
And never never never
Is a long time on your own.

I SING OF
A MAIDEN

Girlish they said I was
And made me Mary, sent me
Packing up the aisle
With Joseph while the shepherds
Gathered at the font
For me to summon them
But first I had to fix the baby
In its crib, my sister's doll
With eyes that closed
And opened, and which bleated
When you laid it down
But no one heard because
O *Little Town* was playing
On the organ *tremolo*
And then I sat down on a stool
With Joseph giving me
A silly smile supposed to look
All holy, and although I tried to do
What I'd been shown, to
Raise an arm, to trace
A glorious arc, a beckoning

Embrace (the shepherds' cue
To get the three of them lined up
And started) all I managed
Was to crook a finger
Nervously until they came.

THE CASE OF SHERLOCK HOLMES

Sherlock Holmes
Is skin and bones
But has a brilliant mind
Which makes it hard
For Scotland Yard
To fall so far behind.

'Why' they grumble
'Did we not stumble
Quicker on this clue?
Even to us
It's obvious
When pointed out by you.'

'You flatter me
But can't you see'
Says Sherlock with a yawn
'That only fools
Go by the rules
While I break every one.

And if you say
I should obey
Each petty regulation,
I do declare
What hope is there
For our glorious British nation?

You know you need
My skill. Agreed?
And I must have my amusement.
I pass the time
By solving crime
But how many hours have *you* spent

Trying to foil
With honest toil
Just one quite clever man
While in a flash
I cut a dash
Through every foolproof plan

And then retreat
To Baker Street,
My pipe and violin,
Until I hear
A knock and dear
Old Mrs. H comes in

To tell me there's
Someone downstairs
Who will not give his name
And so once more
I know for sure
That what's afoot's the game!

So off I go
(Watson in tow –
He's usually around
And always nice
To the police
Who ask *him* what I've found).'

Oh yes, it's hard
For Scotland Yard
To cope with Sherlock's pride.
Do they have cause?
The verdict's yours.
Is he justified?

HOME START

Too big for his boots
so he took to slippers,
shuffled in across the carpet,
put his feet up.

Too clever for words
so he did without them,
pushed to one side
his alphabet soup.

Too pleased with himself
so he said *Can I help you?*
but receiving no answer
went to bed early.

Too old for his years
so he mastered subtraction,
made of a minus
his near horizon.

Too true to be good
so either believe him
or when the wind changes
watch his face.

THE
HUB CAPS

Short of pocket money
Before our holiday,
I asked if I could clean the car
And Dad said *Right, OK.*

Handing me the chamois
(A word I couldn't spell)
He warned *We're taking Granny
So make sure you clean it well,*

*And don't forget the hub caps,
Buff them till they shine.
I want the wheels to spin and say
Now that's a son of mine!*

Turtle-wax the bonnet,
Elbow-grease the boot,
Polish the wing-mirrors
While I plan the route.

Tell me when you've finished
And it's time for my inspection.
There must not be a single spot
Where I can't see my reflection.

I want the rubber, glass and chrome
To glitter, gleam and glow,
And don't forget the hub caps.
OK, then. Off you go!

PUMPKINS IN NEW ENGLAND

All night on lamplit doorsteps
They contained the sun
Then let it out at dawn
And sat there smugly

Or from window-sills
In children's bedrooms
Held plump dialogue
With half a moon.

Without them
Fall would not have come,
Without their pompous troops
Of noisy amber

There could be no Fall –
But now it's winter
And a different story,
Now what are

These witless heads
Abandoned after Halloween,
These mortal bellies
Splitting in the snow?

SLOWLY

Slowly the coming down
For breakfast, pulling back
The curtains in each room, the opening
Of windows just a little (*Have to
Let the air in*), asking me
To pick the letters up
To save him bending, slowly
Reading them, his grey lips
Moving in his beard
To shape each word, then slowly
Walking to his desk
And standing there in front of
Grandma's photo, saying
*Well, old girl, how goes it?
Here's another day!*

Slowly goes everything
In Grandpa's house,
But beautifully too, just right.
He likes us coming.
Mum says it can't go on
Much longer, talks about
Arrangements, but I don't see
Why. The thing to do is
Just what Grandpa says you should,
To take things slowly, very
Slowly till they stop.

THE
LOST VOICE

Your grandpa's lost his voice,
They said. *You mustn't*
Make him try to talk.

And so we sat through tea
While words flew all around him
About this and that...

His eyes kept going back and forth
And side to side as if
He didn't want to miss a syllable

But I knew better. This
Was serious, an old man
Searching for his voice

Who could not find it.

THE
JIGSAW MAN

Do you really think you can
Keep up with the Jigsaw Man
Who sits and thinks and thinks and sits
Surrounded by a sea of bits
Of every shape, of every size,
Then suddenly, with blazing eyes,
Puts this one here and that one there
Yet still, it seems, finds time to spare
To smile at you, to watch your face
As he snaps them into place?
Ah yes, indeed, it may have been
Your idea to challenge him
But he belongs to those who know
Exactly where the pieces go.

A patch of land, a slice of sky,
A tree, a river running by,
The usual scene that you'd expect
With everything present and correct
So why, you wonder, couldn't you
Do what the Jigsaw Man can do
And fit it all inside its frame
Instead of merely feeling shame
When after thinking hard and long
You try a piece and find it's wrong,
Putting land where sky should be.
Oh better leave it all to me
He says, and then the puzzle's done,
The Jigsaw Man has upped and gone
Knowing that now you'll never know
Exactly where the pieces go
And leaving you the dullest bit,
The trouble of undoing it.

THE CAMPAIGN

They gave me the book
I had set my heart on,
A blunt pair of scissors,
A Gripfix carton,
And spread an old newspaper
Over the floor –
Remember the mess
You made before!

I was fingers and thumbs
But expert enough
To marshall the troops
That I cut up rough
And then to admire
How they stood their ground
With a litter of paper-strips
Strewn around.

THE GHOST

If you ever think you see one
There will have to be one

Since nothing can appear
That wasn't here.

A remembered face
Fills its own space

As yours must too,
I promise you.

Some say that time
Is an unsolved crime

But no one ever knows
Where a ghost goes.

NEXT TO NOWHERE

This is my place, this dead-end space
Without a name. I guess
You could call it next to nowhere. No one
Seems to own it, want it, tell me
I can't stay here, and that's why
I like it, why it's getting better
All the time. Its dusty weeds and rubble
Suit my mood if I'm in trouble,
Seem to know exactly how
I feel, don't ever ask me
What's the point?
As if I ought to know.

So this is where I go.
And do I think great thoughts here?
No, no thank you, no
It's just an empty patch of ground
Where I can hang around
And wait and wait and wait
Till nothing happens...

A SONNET FOR MY FATHER'S SON

However many bottles in the cabinet,
Whatever unread books behind the glass,
I knew that I would never play for Somerset,
That children always travel second class.
For all the china on our mantelpiece,
For all the velvet lining in our drawers,
There was no polish without elbow-grease
Or gain except by adding up the scores.
Music stayed put in the piano stool,
Money did not grow on any tree,
And God behaved himself at Sunday School
And holidays were spent beside the sea.
As for the world, I knew it lay in wait,
That there were punishments for being late.

CRUSTIES

Crusties turn in early
And fuss about *The Key*
Or stay up late and worry
Over endless cups of tea.
They seem to think that schoolwork
Should take up all your time –
Pleasure sends them both berserk,
That crusty pair of mine.

They must have once been twenty
(Or even seventeen)
And though The Horn of Plenty
Is not their kind of scene
They shouldn't think one lager
Will change me to a lout –
Oh for a mother/father
Who knows what life's about.

Crusties are couch potatoes
That bake beside the fire
And dream of when you wore nice clothes
And sang in the church choir.
They tell you *Write to Granny*,
They want you young again,
Their deafness is uncanny,
Crusties are a pain.

You cannot make them listen
However hard you try
To get them to see reason
Or half-way eye to eye.
They criticise your music
Because it's played too loud –
Crusties simply make you sick.
They shouldn't be allowed.

So hide inside your earphones
And lock your bedroom door –
The joy of being all alone's
That crusties seem no more
Until one morning when you wake
To find it's dawned on you
There's been a terrible mistake
And you're a crusty too.

THE ANSWER

It's at the back of the book
But you musn't look.

It's underneath a stone
But which one, which one?

It's there at the start
But only in part.

It's not what you know
But it goes where you go.

It's the end of the game
But you're glad you came.

THE THREE-LEGGED PIG

A pair of statesman walking in the world
Saw only what they wanted to until
Their path was crossed by a three-legged pig
Wobbling a little but still coping well.

Good sir, they said, hailing the peasant
Who, proprietorially, followed after.
What a splendid pig you have, but why... ?
He interrupted them with splendid peasant
    laughter.

*Sires, indeed you speak the truth. This pig
Has, in its time, from fire and flood
And other accidents delivered me
In sundry ways. This pig is great and good.*

The statesmen, knowing they beheld a wonder,
Wondered, while the peasant, like a peasant,
   needed to get on.
But why three legs? they asked him. *Why*
So maimed or incompletely formed, your paragon?

He looked at them in turn, amazed, as if to ask
Which of such wise men was the greater dunce
Then answered *When you find a pig as*
   marvellous as this
You don't eat it all at once.

KIM'S GAME

Cut your loss
And leave them here:
The double cross,
The single tear,

The broken promise,
The kept word,
The smile, the kiss,
The little bird,

The sudden thought,
The quick lie,
The hope, the doubt,
The blind eye,

I shall remember
What you bring
For now, for ever,
Everything.

THE LOVE BIRD

Here is a place of broken stones,
Of twisted trees and littered bones,
Of castles barred and turreted
Where knocking could not raise the dead,
Of flowers, each thrusting up a fist
To hammer at the stubborn mist,
Of treacherous paths which seem to wind
Towards what should be left behind.

But here are a prince and princess too
On shining horses riding through
Without suspicion or alarm
Because no wickedness can harm
That bird they carry in its cage
Whose song turns bitterness and rage
And all the grief which lies around
To music on enchanted ground.

LINE UP

Line up for the tuck shop,
Line up for the lab,
Line up at the bus stop,
Line up for your jab.

Line up for examinations,
Line up to to be picked,
Line up just to test your patience,
Line up till you're ticked.

Line up for your dinner,
Line up in the gym,
Line up behind the winner,
Line up in line with him.

Line up to accept your prize,
Line up to receive the cup,
Line up without whats or whys,
Line up, line up, line up.

Line up because we tell you to,
Line up and stand straight.
Line up. Look, how well you do.
Step out of line? The hell you do!
Line up here and wait.

WHO GOES THERE?

Like a cocked rifle
He stands at a sharp angle
To himself, his own
Covering fire.

Anyone can
Trigger him off.
One short burst of him
Is tongue after tongue
Of flame.

Like splinters
His eyes get in
Your eyes.

If he becomes your friend
Be careful who you point him at.

MY MIRROR

When I look in my mirror
The face that I see
Becomes two different voices
That can't agree.

One says; *You're handsome,*
No problem at all.
Whoever you go for
Will come when you call.

The other says; *Lover boy,*
Who are you kidding?
If anyone comes
They'll go without bidding!

It's not that I'm vain
And it's not that I'm blind.
I just want my mirror
To make up its mind.

TO AN OLD MAN SITTING UNDER A CHERRY TREE ON A WINDY AFTERNOON

Nothing on your head
At all,
No hat, no beret,
Scarf or shawl,
No cap, sou'wester,
Just thin hair
To catch the blossom
Drifting there.

EXTRA

Today I come on
near the end, speak
not a word but have to
hang around a lot
and listen looking very
solemn. Somebody
has died and there's
this poetry going
on and on about
how if he'd lived etc.
then there's trumpets
and a cannon then
more poetry. Yesterday
I ran across the stage
at the beginning with
a word or two in prose
and lots of laughter. Comedies
are best because you
get to say *Odds bodkins*
or a *Sire* or two
and if you don't stand still
it doesn't matter. *Will,*
I keep on asking him,
can I audition for a
larger part, and when
shall I be ready
for my first soliloquy?

But all he's done just lately
is to mutter, with a hand up
to that noble brow
and with a distant look,
Tomorrow and tomorrow
and tomorrow, or
in other words
get lost. Patience,
I tell myself, the man's
a genius, your time
will come. Just now
he must have
something very heavy
on his mind.

THE TEAM GAME

Every team game has a whistle
And the whistle blows for you
A shriek of imminent dismissal
Or a shrill of ballyhoo
For what you've done or ought to do.

Across the pitch the Ref comes thundering,
Trouble with a darkened brow,
While you just stand there, palely wondering
When the why and why the how
Became where not to do this now.

He takes his little yellow book out,
Licks a stumpy pencil stub
Then warns you that you'd better look out,
Knuckle down and join the club
Or get cold-shouldered, sent off, snubbed.

And so the game goes on. You follow
Those who clearly know the score
But whose expressions seem to borrow
Time from the team that played before –
They make no fresh moves any more.

It's all a risk. You have to run one.
You must either learn to play –
Passing the same old rules to someone –
Or seize the whistle, disobey,
And blow it. There's no other way.

WHAT
REALLY HAPPENED

Humpty Dumpty
Sat in the corner
While Litle Jack Horner
Sat on a wall
But Little Miss Muffet
Stayed on her tuffet,
Not being frightened
Of spiders at all.

WHAT A LOT I GOT

Sometimes when people tell you things
It's hard to know what to say –
Like the little girl with her hair in rings
Who came up to me yesterday.

She tugged at my corduroy jacket
To make sure I'd bend down to hear,
Then as if she meant to attack it
She shouted these words in my ear.

I've got fifteen verucas.
(She had counted them last night in bed.)
I could think of no rhyme for verucas
So *Jolly well done!* I said.

BY THE SOUND OF IT

To wake at night
And find the day not ended yet

For everyone, although
It's obviously time to go

As hurrying feet tap by
Attached to somebody

Who slams a car-door,
Drives off with a roar

And then the lights go out
Like plucking fruit

From darkness, one by one,
Until the last has gone

And left just me
Attached to somebody

Who cannot sleep
Because of a sudden hush so deep

It roars and echoes in his ears
As if for years.

MILKFLOAT

A stuttering whine
At crack of dawn
Before the earliest
Curtain's drawn.

It stops, it starts,
It stops again,
It starts, it stops,
It starts again.

And then at last
It goes away,
Rattling its crates
At break of day.

SEPTEMBER

Come back from summer
To your own absence,
The curtains drawn
And nobody at home.

A sudden hesitation
On the doorstep –
Have you been
Too long away?

The lights are out,
The window box is empty,
Neighbours pass
But do not say a word.

Only the hidden key
Is where you left it.
Open up,
Remember who you are.

GIACOMETTI

(for Ben – who admires his sculpture)

Gia
co
met
ti
ate
spa
gh
ett
i
dra
nk
Chi
an
ti
too
b
ut
sta
y
ed
as
thi
n
as
Ben
ja
min
as
mo
st
gre
at
art
is
ts
DO

THE IMPROVING BOOK

Please accept this book
Which comes with our love
And the earnest hope
You'll want to read it.

Needless to say
There are no pictures
But we recommend
The very useful index.

You must not judge it
By the cover.
There's room for improvement
In all our lives.

Many there are
The better for it
Though they couldn't tell you
How or why.

We've sent your brother
Arthur Ransome
Who, so we're told,
Has always gone down well.

WHAT'S WRONG
WITH THE CHILD?

The tick has a tock in it,
The phone has a lock on it,
Nobody cares about me.
The sky's the wrong colour,
The ditchwater's duller
And Rachel is coming to tea.

But my bedroom, I'm free in it,
The lock has a key in it,
Everyone leaves me alone.
I shall pull back the curtain
To make double certain
That Rachel is on her way home.

A Christmas Apparition

Down at the bottom of my bed
Was Herod, standing on his head.
He waved his big feet in the air.
I heard him cry *It isn't fair* –

If I'd known then what I now know
About that little so-and-so
I'd be the right way up tonight
And walking tall and clothed in light

Instead of this. I heard him groan.
Those feet looked terribly alone
As if, for all his loud self-mocking,
They'd never fit my Christmas stocking.

THE OTHER SHEPHERD

Oh let them be, he muttered,
Let them plan their journey,
Let that brilliant interrupting stranger
Beckon them to Bethlehem.
A little fling won't hurt them,
A change of air might suit them,
Get this twitch out of their system
But they'll soon be back.

So then he broke a loaf
And drained a goatskin, then,
The wine still wet upon his lips
And sparkling in his beard like stars,
He nodded off...

Tired men prefer
Sleep to a great wonder.

THE BOSS

He checked his wrist
To see if he could
Make it, always
In a hurry, racing
Against time

Until his urgency
Became a habit
And he grew old
Winding up the clocks.

LUCKY SUMS

One plus one is two
And two plus two is four
When love plus luck plus you
Arrive at my front door.

But one from four leaves three
And three from four leaves one
While love from luck leaves me
Afraid you may not come.

Then two times four makes eight
And three times three makes nine
So love times luck times fate
Times you must equal MINE!

Two into ten goes five,
Five into ten goes two...
Oh I am the luckiest boy alive
Whose sums all end with you.

MR PUNCH

Did he have friends
When he was a kid?
Oh no he didn't.
Oh yes he did.

Was he ever upset
When his mum got so cross?
Oh no he wasn't.
Oh yes he was.

Had he frightened his sister
And laughed at his dad?
Oh no he hadn't.
Oh yes he had.

Should he learn manners
And try to be good?
Oh no he shouldn't.
Oh yes he should.

Does he go calling
Policemen *The Fuzz*?
Oh no he doesn't.
Oh yes he does.

When he is told to
Will he sit still?
Oh no he won't.
Oh yes he will.

Has he made up with Judy
Or turned down his jazz?
Oh no he hasn't.
Oh yes he has.

If he tried to explain
Would he be understood?
Oh no he wouldn't.
Oh yes he would.

Or must he stay always
A man we can't trust?
Oh no he mustn't.
Oh yes he must.

PLAYTIME

The simple guns have nothing to pretend.
We go to bed at eight, each night the same.
Over abandoned toys our mothers bend.

All that is broken let our fathers mend.
What leaves the nusery that we can't reclaim?
The simple guns have nothing to pretend.

This boy who fires the match-sticks is my friend.
We don't admit the accidental flame.
Over abandoned toys our mothers bend.

His rash intention is what I intend.
We knew each other the first time he came.
The simple guns have nothing to pretend.

But our pretence is why our people send
Each to the other's house. We play their game.
Over abandoned toys our mothers bend.

It's anybody's guess how this will end.
Each time we say *hello* we're taking aim.
The simple guns have nothing to pretend.
Over abandoned toys our mothers bend.

MISTAKEN IDENTITY

It wasn't me
Who came in late,
Who slammed the door,
Who slept so long,
Who got it wrong,
Who wanted more,
Who had to wait.
It wasn't me.

It wasn't you
Who shrank from touch,
Who cried all night,
Who rang the school,
Who felt a fool,
Who looked a sight,
Who drank too much.
It wasn't you.

It wasn't us
Who smiled in vain,
Who built the wall,
Who piled each stone,
Who ate alone,
Who bore the pain,
Who lost it all.
It wasn't us.

MY SIDE OF THE BARGAIN

Half of a room
Is better than none
So I'll give you the moon
But you can't have the sun.
I'm keeping the lolly,
You're getting the stick,
And I'm feeling as jolly
As you're feeling sick!

You can look at that chair
But you're not sitting in it,
You can stand over there
But for less than a minute,
I'm counting the seconds,
I'm watching the clock,
And I just about reckon
You've ticked your last tock!

Oh half of a room
Is more than a quarter,
And a very long spoon
Will make your meal shorter,
So come in if I let you
Then go when I say,
And if I forget you
Remember to pay.

HOP FROG

Hop Frog, Hop Frog, never stop frog,
Never settled in one place,
Always leaping into trouble
With that frog smile on your face.

Could it be you're tired of waiting
For the world to change its tune?
Sitting still seems wasted effort,
Soon enough is not too soon.

When I look at you I wonder
Why not dive and disappear?
Have we both outstayed our welcome?
One last leap would see us clear.

But that smile is all your answer,
All that it was meant to be –
Hop Frog, Hop Frog, never stop frog,
Leave us guessing, set us free.

WORDS

come out
like stars sometimes
and choose the darkest nights
to sparkle in,

are gentle
water-drops suggesting
streams you cannot find the source of
in a landscape where no
water is,

or wasps
behind your back which
suddenly
go silent.